Smithsonian

ARCHIE
STRIKES GOLD

BY BRANDON TERRELL

ILLUSTRATED BY EVA MORALES

STONE ARCH BOOKS

a capstone imprint

Archie Strikes Gold is published by Stone Arch Books,
an imprint of Capstone.

1710 Roe Crest Drive
North Mankato, Minnesota 56003
www.capstonepub.com

The name of the Smithsonian Institution and the sunburst logo
are registered trademarks of the Smithsonian Institution. For more
information, please visit www.si.edu.

Library of Congress Cataloging-in-Publication Data is available on
the Library of Congress website
ISBN: 978-1-4965-9864-6 (library binding)
ISBN: 978-1-4965-9872-1 (paperback)
ISBN: 978-1-4965-9868-4 (ebook PDF)

Summary: Archie is traveling with his uncle Harold to perform for
those prospecting for gold. While there, Harold befriends an older
gentleman, Montgomery Wycroft, who is in the area prospecting for
gold. Archie and his uncle opt to stay behind in Dawson City, joining
Monty on his dangerous quest for gold, battling with both greedy
gold-seekers and the unforgiving Canadian terrain. Will Archie and
his uncle strike gold, or will they find something more valuable?

Designer: Tracy McCabe

Our very special thanks to Megan Smith, Senior Creative Developer,
Office of Audience Engagement, National Museum of American
History, Smithsonian. Capstone would also like to thank Kealy
Gordon, Product Development Manager, and the following at
Smithsonian Enterprises: Jill Corcoran, Director, Licensed Publishing;
Brigid Ferraro, Vice President, Education and Consumer Products; and
Carol LeBlanc, President, Smithsonian Enterprises.

Printed in the United States of America.
PA117

TABLE OF CONTENTS

Chapter 1
A Dangerous Path.................. 5

Chapter 2
Music in Dawson City 17

Chapter 3
Up at Bonanza Creek 31

Chapter 4
Striking Gold! 41

Chapter 5
Finding Home 53

Chapter 1

A Dangerous Path

June 1898
Dyea, Alaska

Archie Clifton hefted the pack onto his back and felt its straps dig into his shoulder blades. At eleven years old, he was thin, and the pack was weighed down with a full canteen, bricks of food, and a supply of clothes.

"How long is the trail?" Archie asked his uncle Harold, with whom he was traveling. Harold had been Archie's guardian ever since his parents had died when he was eight.

The snowy path in front of them wove through dense evergreen trees covered with snow. Goods and supplies in brown burlap sacks and wooden crates were stacked on either side of the path. A long line of people—mostly men—climbed the trail, pulling sleds behind them.

Uncle Harold tied a thick rope to the sled of supplies in front of him. He ran a dirty hand through his slicked-back brown hair. "Long," he replied. "Chilkoot Trail is more than thirty miles."

"Thirty-three miles of misery, to be exact," said a stocky, thick-bearded man named Dutch. Uncle Harold had met Dutch on the steamship from Seattle. The bearded man had agreed to let the two of them join him and his crew.

"More men equals less weight to carry," Dutch had explained.

Archie grimaced at Dutch's comment. "Remind me again why we're doing this," he said.

Uncle Harold flashed a smile. "Gold, my boy," he replied.

It seemed like a dangerous gamble to come all this way with the slim hope of getting rich. But Uncle Harold was a determined man. Once he saw an opportunity he liked, he did everything he could to obtain it. Archie recalled the day back in Seattle, a year or so ago, when Uncle Harold had waved a newspaper in his face, showing him the headline: "GOLD! GOLD! GOLD! GOLD!"

The steamship *Portland* had just docked, back from the Klondike in Canada. The article stated that its arrival was met by thousands of poor, desperate people aching to see a little nugget of hope. What they saw was a ship full of it—jars and crates and bags of gold.

Uncle Harold was not a miner. His fingers didn't dig holes. Instead, they tickled the ivories of a piano. Archie played his fiddle alongside Uncle Harold at saloons—bars—and theaters across the state of Washington. But money had been sparse lately. Jobs were hard to come by. And just like everyone else who'd spied that ship of treasure, Uncle Harold had eventually gotten the itch for more.

So here they were, about to climb a cold mountain pass on their way to a Yukon town called Dawson City.

"Away we go," Uncle Harold said. He swung the thick rope over his shoulder and pulled the sled behind him.

Archie and his uncle joined Dutch's crew and the swarm of people on the trail. Many of them were like Archie: lean, wiry, and unfit for the perils the path offered. Soon, the boy was panting and wishing he could simply scoop a handful of snow and eat it. But according to the flyer he'd been handed as they prepared their sled with goods, that was a bad idea. Snow should be melted first before being eaten. The pamphlet had also offered advice like: "Do not waste an ounce of anything," and "No man can drag more than his weight."

This made Archie glance down at the sled his uncle was pulling. Though they obviously could not take Uncle Harold's prized piano with them, they did have Archie's fiddle. Its black, dented case sat atop the supplies on the sled. It rattled back and forth with each pull.

The journey was long. Because each person was expected to carry a year's worth of food and supplies to live in the Yukon, the group traveled to one spot, dropped their goods, and retraced their steps to get more of their belongings. At points, the winding trail was narrow and treacherous. Many nights, Archie would shrug off his pack and slump down before the campfire with his leg muscles burning and aching, too tired to play the fiddle.

"Keep your head down and your feet moving," Uncle Harold would repeat every time Archie felt himself slowing down. "Always moving."

***

Finally they reached a long, uphill climb between two mountains. Small human-made steps were carved into the ice and snow, with a coarse guide rope stretched along one side for support. Archie heard one of the men in Dutch's crew—a tall, lean fella named Frankie—call it the "Golden Staircase."

The crew made the trek to the trail's peak—more than a thousand steps. When they reached the top, Archie knew they'd have to go back down for more supplies.

As Archie prepared to join the men, Dutch slapped a hand on the stack of provisions.

"You stay here," Dutch told him. "We'll get the rest."

Archie's tired legs needed a break. He didn't protest as Uncle Harold and the others disappeared back down the Golden Staircase.

Archie sat among the throng of men and their supplies. He took out his fiddle and began to play. The sweet music drifted across the air, the twisting notes slipping into the shadows and dancing through pine trees. Men stopped in front of Archie. They closed their eyes and tapped their boots in the snow.

"That's beautiful," one man said. Tears had formed in his eyes. "Been a long time since I heard music."

Another man placed a hunk of dried meat on the crate next to Archie. "Thanks, kid," he said.

When Uncle Harold and the rest of the crew returned with all their goods, Archie set the fiddle back in its case. He was saddened by the loss of noise. The world felt quiet and dark without music.

At long last, the group reached the end of the Chilkoot Trail. Their reward was a scene unlike any Archie had imagined. A beautiful lake stretched across the horizon. Its crystal blue water looked like a sheet of glass.

"Lake Bennett," Uncle Harold said. He inhaled deeply and then let his breath out slowly through his nose.

Dutch clapped Uncle Harold on the back. "Ain't she a beaut?" he asked Archie.

"Sure is," Archie answered.

"No time to rest, though." Dutch nodded at their supplies. Frankie and a few others were already sorting lumber from it, along with another crew of men who had also just reached the serene lake. "We've got a boat to make," he said.

"A boat?" Archie was confused. "We're not at Dawson City?"

Dutch shook his head. "Not even close. We've gotta build ourselves a boat and take it downriver. Then we'll be at Dawson."

Archie couldn't seem to get his jaw to close. All this time, and they weren't even at their destination?

"Hurry along," Dutch said. "Boat ain't gonna build itself, is it?"

Chapter 2

Music in Dawson City

The boat they made on the shores of Lake Bennett was primitive—just oak wood held together by pitch and nails. They weren't the only ones casting off down the Yukon River on a leaky raft. All the potential miners had to do the same. Eight men, plus Archie, would be traveling on their makeshift boat.

They packed the boat with provisions and floated downriver on a hope and a prayer.

The water was icy cold. It splashed across the boat's deck, soaking into Archie's boots.

Dutch and his men did their best to steer the craft. The river had other ideas, though. Its current led them on their way.

Several days into the journey, they reached an area of churning rapids. "Hold steady!" Dutch bellowed.

The boat bucked and swayed. Waves crashed on all sides. A crate of supplies toppled from the boat, splashing into the river and sinking to its frigid depths. Archie saw the broken remains of other boats along the shoreline and did his best not to think of what had happened to the boats' crews.

Frankie stumbled back. He slammed an elbow into Archie's stomach.

Archie fell back toward the water!

"Help!" he cried out. His arms flailed, reaching for something—*anything*—to grasp. But there was nothing to stop his fall. He would crash into the water, be pulled by the

undertow, and slammed against the boulders at the river's edge.

"I've got you!"

Uncle Harold's arm lashed out. It gripped the front of Archie's coat just in time. Dutch reached over and his strong arms pulled Archie safely back onto the makeshift boat. Archie righted himself. His cold hands shook. His teeth chattered.

"Th-th-thanks," he said, staggering to the center of the boat and sitting among the crates of supplies to stay safe.

***

That night, as they camped on the shore, Archie slept close to the fire, warming his wet socks and boots. He did his best to be brave and not think about the incident on the boat.

"Just keep moving," he said to himself, remembering Uncle Harold's words. "Always moving."

***

Days later, as the boat glided smoothly downstream while the afternoon sun gleamed overhead, Archie looked up and saw a large mountain with what looked like a scar at its center. In its shadow was a bustling town, buildings with smoke curling from their chimneys, and streets lined with people.

Archie pointed. "Look!" he shouted.

"Dawson City!" Dutch cried out. He ripped the stocking cap from his head. The men onboard the makeshift boat cheered. Their whoops and hollers echoed across the clear blue sky. They hugged one another triumphantly.

They'd made it. After all the peril and adventure through the mountains and down the river, the crew had successfully arrived at Dawson City.

***

Archie stepped out from the ramshackle room he and Uncle Harold rented at the Dawson City Inn. In one hand he held his fiddle case. He hustled down the hall, past a series of closed doors. Behind them, miners snored loudly.

Archie burst from the inn's front door and out into the street as the church bells chimed nine a.m. He was late. Uncle Harold was already at the saloon, no doubt tapping his foot and wondering where Archie could be.

It had been nearly a month since they'd arrived in Dawson City. Archie was still trying to get used to their surroundings, to their new life. He wasn't sure how long they'd be staying.

"Excuse me," Archie said. "Coming through." He ran along the dirt-packed street, weaving between men in thick coats and wide-brimmed hats. They all looked the same: the same hat, the same dirty coat, the same mustache, even.

The men and women of Dawson City were known as "stampeders," named for the way they'd stampeded to the Yukon in search of gold. The streets were filled with them.

Since the first gold was found last year, the population of the town had exploded. Thousands of people made their home in Dawson City now—so many that almost all the buildings were temporary ones, built after the gold rush had begun.

A dog barked at Archie as he raced past a mercantile and a clothing store. The ringing sounds of metal on metal clanged from the blacksmith's shop. The constant sound of hammering filled the air.

The saloon was straight ahead. Sure enough, Archie could see his uncle on the wooden porch out front.

"Strike of nine, Archie, my boy," Uncle Harold said.

"Sorry, sir," Archie replied. He joined his uncle, setting his fiddle case on the wooden slats at his feet and opening it. He took out the instrument.

"Mr. Thatcher needs me manning the piano inside," Uncle Harold said, "and you out here, bringing in customers with that fiddle of yours." Like many saloons, this one was open all hours, day and night. Uncle Harold played during the day, relieving the night pianist.

Uncle Harold had taken the roughly seven-mile trek up to Bonanza Creek several times, leaving Archie to fiddle on the streets for the day. But since there were so many people panning for gold, Uncle Harold had yet to land himself with a crew for an extended period of time. So he played the piano and waited for his chance.

Uncle Harold straightened the ratty coat he'd bought at the small clothing store, turned, and strode through the swinging doors.

A moment later, the sound of tinkling piano keys drifted from the saloon.

Archie nestled his fiddle under his chin and began to play.

As the morning wore on, Archie's music drew the men and women of Dawson City to his side of the gravel street. Some tossed coins into his open fiddle case. A few others left flakes and small nuggets of gold.

That was one thing Archie had noticed about several of the stampeders. Whatever gold they found in the Yukon was going to *stay* in the Yukon. They immediately spent the money they made. Not Archie and Uncle Harold. They saved whatever small pittance they made from their music. And when they were on a crew, they were likely to do the very same thing.

By early afternoon, the autumn sun was high in the sky. Archie had a modest amount of money in his case and a rumbling in his belly. He gathered his coins into the pocket of his coat and stored his fiddle in its case.

When he looked up, he saw a boy about his age sitting on a stack of crates, watching him. The boy wore a shirt and dusty overalls, with one knee torn.

"Where ya goin'?" the boy asked.

"Get some soup," Archie replied. "Why?"

The boy shrugged. "Seen ya out here before," he said. "You ain't bad."

"Gee, thanks."

The boy hopped down off the crate and walked up to Archie. He took off his cap, revealing blond hair about the same length as Archie's. "Just saying, you're pretty good."

"Yeah, well, I only feel comfortable when I'm playing it." Archie rapped his knuckles on the dented fiddle case. "Makes me feel like I'm back home."

"You miss home?"

"A little."

"Not me."

Archie's stomach rumbled again. "Listen, fella," he said. "It's nice to meet you, but I really got to get something to eat."

The new kid's lips curled into a sneer. "Fella? Who you callin' *fella*?"

It wasn't until then that Archie took a close look at the kid. He wasn't a boy after all but a young girl with dirty cheeks and hard eyes.

"Sorry," Archie muttered.

"Better be." The girl gave Archie a shove, knocking him back. The fiddle case fell hard to the gravel, skittering away from him.

The girl balled her hands into fists. It looked like she was going to fight Archie. Instead, she stormed away in a huff.

"Hey!" Archie hollered. But the girl disappeared into a crowd of stampeders.

"Archie, my boy!" Uncle Harold's voice rang out from behind him. "What are you doing on the ground?"

Archie turned to see his uncle exiting the saloon with an older man. The man's face was a map of deep creases and wrinkles. A bushy mustache hid his mouth, from which an unlit cigar stuck out.

Archie quickly stood and brushed the dust from his trousers. "Nothing, sir," he said.

"Well, I've got good news." Uncle Harold flashed him a smile. "Our musical days are over. For now, at least. I'd like you to meet Monty Wycroft."

Archie nodded. "Pleasure to meet you," he said.

"Ol' Monty here has asked us to join his crew up at Bonanza," Uncle Harold explained. "Archie, my boy, we're officially gold miners!"

Chapter 3

Up at Bonanza Creek

"Welcome to Bonanza!" Monty Wycroft said the next morning. His gravelly voice echoed through the trees.

Archie and his uncle had just joined the crew of miners at the creek northwest of Dawson City. Bonanza Creek, an offshoot of the Klondike River, wound its way through thick pines and rocky outcroppings.

Archie blew into his hands. Unlike the warmth of Dawson City, the autumn chill was strong in the shadows of the creek. Behind them, a long, narrow log cabin had been constructed.

"This claim is all yours?" Dutch asked with wide-eyed wonder.

After Uncle Harold had proclaimed them gold miners, he had sought out his old traveling companions to see if they were interested as well. Dutch, who had been working in construction, immediately said yes. Frankie had signed on too.

"Every claim on Bonanza has been staked," Monty explained, another unlit cigar bouncing in his mouth. When he saw Archie's puzzled look, he added, "A claim is a parcel of land. Only my men and I can mine it. There are more than five hundred claims on this creek alone." He waved one hand. "Let me show you the operation."

As Monty began to walk toward the shoreline, the cabin door banged open. "Grandpop!" a voice shouted. "Wait up!"

Archie turned and was shocked to see the

girl he'd met the day before running toward them. She wore the same clothes, the same cap hiding her short hair.

"You gotta be kidding me," Archie mumbled.

The girl rushed to Monty's side. She looked over, recognized Archie, and gave him the same sneer she'd thrown his way outside the saloon.

"Everyone, this is my granddaughter Valerie," Monty said. "Val, these boys are gonna help us out."

"Fantastic," Val said with little enthusiasm.

Monty led them to the creek, where a long, narrow, wooden box jutted out from the water. Several men were shoveling gravel into the box while others rocked it back and forth.

"This here is a sluice box," Monty explained. "You scoop up sand and grit, run water down it, and the small bits wash away."

Archie peered into the sluice box. A series of ridges on the bottom were catching larger pieces of earth and stone.

Monty stepped up beside him. "The riffles on the bottom are where the gold gets trapped," he explained.

"What's that?" Dutch nodded toward what looked to Archie like a baby's cradle.

"A rocker box," Monty said.

It was an accurate name. A square, wooden box sat atop what looked like the curved rails at the bottom of a rocking chair.

A man from Monty's crew approached. He was stocky and strong and carried a shovel slung over his shoulder.

Monty took his unlit cigar from his mouth and pointed at the man. "Donald here will help you with the rest. Time to roll up those sleeves and get to work."

With that, Monty strolled away, leaving the men to pan for gold.

***

That night, as the sun dipped below the trees, Frankie and a few others lit a campfire outside the log cabin. The men sat on tree trunks and sprawled in the grass. Archie sat on a stump next to Uncle Harold.

Monty Wycroft stoked the flames, then rested on a fallen log across the fire from Archie. He looked peaceful. Like mining for gold was what he'd always been meant to do.

"So, Monty," Dutch said. He was sitting in the grass, his back leaning against a log. "How'd you stake this patch of beauty?"

"A little bit of luck," Monty answered. "'Course, miners live on luck. What we do is a gamble, ain't it?"

The men around the campfire agreed.

"Most people who come to the Yukon walk away without a flake of gold," Monty explained. "I was one of the first miners to reach the Klondike. Just after George Washington Carmack and the Taglish found gold here."

Archie thought back to his and Uncle Harold's harrowing trip along the Chilkoot Trail. He pictured Monty and Val making the same journey.

"How did you get here?" he asked.

"White Pass Trail from Skagway," Monty said. "White Pass is the other trail to Lake Bennett. Not as steep as Chilkoot, but longer by eleven miles. We were gonna take Chilkoot, but word came back of an avalanche in the mountains. Sixty-plus men gone, buried under the snow."

A chill ran up Archie's spine. He thought of the dangerous pass. An avalanche would make a trip infinitely harder.

"We lost a few pack horses along the way," Monty concluded, "but came out all right."

A silence fell over the team. Only the crackle of the fire filled it. Val stood, walked to the cabin, and came back a moment later. She held Archie's fiddle case.

She handed it to him. "Here," she said. "Play us a song, new kid."

Archie looked at the men and saw them all staring back at him. They seemed to want a song too. So he took out the fiddle and began to play.

Archie's heart swelled as his notes carried into the black sky. The splash of stars looked down on him, watching his fingers and bow dance across the strings.

When Archie had finished his song, the men clapped. Frankie whistled softly. Dutch asked for another song.

Archie felt more at peace than he had since he'd left Seattle.

He readied his fiddle, rested the bow on the taut strings, and was about to play when—

Gunshots rang out into the night!

Chapter 4

Striking Gold!

The men around the campfire were instantly alert. They stood up quickly. Archie dropped the fiddle from his chin, checking to make sure Uncle Harold was all right. He was.

Monty peered into the blackness of the woods. The old prospector took his granddaughter by the hand. "Get to the cabin," he said. "You'll be safe." He pointed at Archie. "You too."

Archie looked toward his uncle, who nodded in agreement.

Several men raced to the cabin. They returned with kerosene lanterns and passed them out. Uncle Harold got one. So did Dutch and Frankie. Other men cradled shotguns in their arms.

Monty led the men into the woods while Archie followed Val toward the cabin. As they neared it, the girl grabbed him by the wrist. "This way," she said, running toward the woods instead.

Archie had no time to protest. He clutched his fiddle tightly as they plunged into the darkness.

If it weren't for the moonlight, Archie would not have been able to see where he was going. Twigs cracked under his feet, and branches scraped at his face and arms. They didn't have to travel far, though. Soon, they saw the glow of the lanterns.

"Shhh!" Val put a finger to her lips. The two of them crept closer to the lantern light.

"They were warning shots!" a man yelled. He was as thin as the dead trees around him. In his hand was a large revolver.

Monty spoke calmly to the man. "I told ya before, Billingham. I got a rightful stake to this claim."

"That's Sam Billingham," Val whispered into Archie's ear, startling him. Her breath smelled sweet, like apples. "He's got the claim next to Grandpop. Hasn't struck gold on it, though."

"I had it before you!" Billingham waggled a finger at Monty. "It's mine, and you know it! Thought I saw your boys coming to sabotage me, so I fired into the air to scare 'em off!"

The man stepped forward menacingly. As he did, Uncle Harold placed himself between the angry prospector and Monty. Archie gasped. His heart thudded in his chest. If anything happened to Uncle Harold . . .

"I think it's time we went our separate ways," Uncle Harold said.

Monty nodded. "Go on back home, Sam," he told Billingham.

"The Yukon is a dangerous place," he warned them. "Never know what kinda accidents can happen," Billingham said. He spat on the ground at Uncle Harold's feet, holstered the revolver, and strode away.

"We gotta get back before they do," Val whispered, tiptoeing cautiously back toward the cabin.

With his fiddle case pressed to his thundering chest, Archie followed.

***

Months passed. Cold, unforgiving months. Winter in the Yukon meant swirling snow and frozen, hard-packed earth. Bonanza Creek never truly iced over, and the men toiled at the sluice box when they could. They shoveled gravel into it and washed it away with the frigid creek water.

Archie and Val spent their days helping where they could. They carried the flakes of gold caught in the riffles of the box to the cabin. They helped cook by dropping a brick of chili into a pot of water boiling over the campfire for the evening meal.

They would also operate the rocker box. Sometimes, if they wanted a moment of peace, they would sneak away from camp, kneel on the creek's shoreline with thin metal pans, and sift for gold on their own. Or form snowballs out of the dirty, wet powder, and throw them at each other.

Archie and his uncle spent the holidays in the warmth of the Wycroft cabin, taking the occasional trip back to Dawson City. He and his uncle exchanged gifts they'd bought for each other in the mercantile shop. Uncle Harold gave Archie a new wool sweater and bow strings for his fiddle. Archie gave his uncle a scuffed compass.

Finally, the world around them thawed. On an afternoon so sunny they could at last shed their heavy coats and stocking caps, Archie and Val snatched a pair of pans and disappeared down the claim. They found a small outcropping of rock and set their pans and canteens on it.

"So, new kid," Val said, sitting on the rock and swinging her legs. "You still miss home?"

Archie hadn't thought about Seattle, not since the day he'd met Val, when she'd shoved him into the dirt for calling her a boy. He'd enjoyed the time he'd spent out at Bonanza Creek, sleeping in a cot in the cabin alongside all the other crew. He considered them family.

Archie shook his head. "No," he said. "Not anymore."

He took a metal pan and knelt in the sand. The water soaked into his trousers at the knees, but Archie didn't mind. He scooped a load of gravel, shaking the pan and sifting the small bits from it.

All that was left were a bunch of big rocks. No gold.

He tried again. And again, he came away with nothing.

His third pan was different.

Archie saw the glint right away. Sure

enough, when he sifted out the grit, there among the rocks was the biggest hunk of gold he'd seen yet!

"Val!" He plucked the nugget from the pan. "I did it! I struck gold!"

Val hopped off the rock and hurried over to join him. "Lemme see!" she said eagerly.

Archie held out his palm. The nugget was the size of an acorn.

Val swiped it from him. "Hey!" he shouted.

She gazed closely at it, then took a pocketknife from her trousers. With the knife, she carved the letter *V* roughly into the gold.

"There," she said with a smile, showing him the nugget. "I've claimed this now!"

Before Archie could reply, he suddenly heard frantic shouts in the distance. The sound of the sluice box stopped.

Archie stood and looked back toward the direction of camp. Thick, black smoke billowed over the treetops!

Chapter 5

Finding Home

"Look, Val!" Archie yelled.

Val craned her head toward the dense, black smoke. Her eyes widened.

The gold forgotten, the two of them left the metal pans on the shoreline and ran as fast as they could back toward the camp. Archie swatted away tree branches and leaped over fallen logs.

"Fire!" Dutch bellowed just as Archie and Val burst from the trees and out into the clearing.

The sight stopped Archie in his tracks. The cabin was engulfed in flames. The blaze licked the log walls and danced in the windows. Archie could feel its heat even from where he stood, more than a hundred yards away.

"Grandpop!" Val screamed. She brushed past Archie and ran toward the crew. Some were trying to douse the flames with buckets of water from the creek. But it was hopeless. Even Archie could see that.

Monty stood among the men. He turned at the sound of his name and nearly collapsed when he saw Val was safe. "My dear," he uttered. "I thought you were inside."

Archie searched the crew for Uncle Harold. He was nowhere to be seen.

"Billingham's to blame," Monty said with a scowl. "Can't prove it, but I know it was him."

Archie cupped his hands to his mouth. "Uncle Harold!" he yelled.

"He went inside to look for you!" Dutch hollered back, pointing at the cabin.

Then, from the billowing plumes of black smoke at the rear of the cabin, Uncle Harold appeared like a mirage. He staggered forward, waving his arms. "Archie!" he yelled. "Where are you? I didn't see you inside." He burst into a fit of coughing.

"Here! I'm here, Uncle Harold! I'm safe!"

When he saw Archie, Uncle Harold's eyes widened. He stumbled over. His face was covered in soot, and parts of his left sleeve had been singed off.

Uncle Harold took Archie in his arms and hugged him fiercely. "I thought I'd lost you, boy," he said.

"You didn't," Archie assured him. "You didn't."

Archie watched as the men continued working, trying to smother the flames.

Suddenly a thought hit him like a blow to the stomach.

"My fiddle," he whispered. Tears burned in the corners of his eyes, and he hugged his uncle tighter. It was gone. His home, in more ways than one, had been destroyed.

***

That night, in a hotel room back in Dawson City, where Monty Wycroft's tired and soot-covered crew had been forced to sleep, Uncle Harold came up to Archie's cot. He leaned down.

"Tomorrow," he whispered, "I'm taking you out of here."

***

Just before sunrise, Uncle Harold shook Archie awake. "Steamship leaves for Lake Bennett soon," he said.

There was nothing to pack. Nearly their

entire lives had been inside what was now a smoldering heap of ash and ruin.

It felt strange, leaving without saying goodbye. But when Archie thought of the way Uncle Harold had looked at him through the smoke, he understood. Despite the friendships they'd made in the Yukon, Uncle Harold was his only true family member. And he'd devoted his life to keeping Archie safe.

From the moment they'd set foot on Chilkoot Trail, they'd discovered the life of a miner was dangerous. But it was the fire that made them each realize that some things are more important than gold.

As they stepped out of the inn and into the crisp spring morning, Archie noticed Monty Wycroft sitting on a stool nearby. He was studying a map, like he was already plotting out how best to rebuild.

"Harold," Monty said. Archie could tell by

the tone in his voice that Monty knew they were leaving.

"Sorry to do this to you, Mr. Wycroft," Uncle Harold said.

Monty stood up and looked at them. The smell of smoke was still pungent between the three of them. For a moment, Archie wasn't sure how Monty was going to react. Then the old prospector thrust out his hand for Uncle Harold to shake.

"We sure are gonna miss you fellas," Monty said.

Uncle Harold shook his hand, followed by Archie. "Us too, sir," he said.

Monty dug into his pocket and drew out a handful of gold. "May your travels be safe," he said, passing along the gold to Uncle Harold.

Uncle Harold nodded.

"Is . . . is Val awake?" Archie asked. "I really want to say goodbye."

Monty shook his head. "Haven't seen her this morning, son. I'll give her your best."

"Thank you, sir," Archie replied sadly.

Archie and Uncle Harold walked down the gravel path toward the harbor. Even at this early hour, the streets of Dawson City were buzzing. A new locomotive was rumored to be opening at Lake Bennett soon, bringing even more men and women to the Yukon. In just a few short years, the area had gone from a secret to a booming destination. Soon, though, there'd be other places to go, other treasures to seek.

A steamship waited on the shore of the Yukon River. It made Archie think of the ramshackle raft they'd taken to get to Dawson City. Since then, ships like the one they were about to board had carried many more people back and forth along the Yukon. The return voyage to Seattle would be much less perilous, thankfully.

"Wait up a sec!"

Archie turned. Val was dashing down the street. When she reached them, she skidded to a stop.

"You were gonna leave without saying goodbye?" she asked.

"Sorry," Archie said. "Your grandpa said you weren't around. I didn't wanna leave without . . . ," he trailed off.

Val punched him lightly on the shoulder. "Gonna miss you," she said.

"Yeah. I'll miss you too."

Val took a small leather pouch from her trouser pocket and handed it to him. "A going-away gift," she said.

Archie could see tears welling up in her eyes, but Val used a sleeve to brush them away.

"Thanks," Archie said. He felt guilty that he had nothing to give her in return.

"Yeah, well . . ." Val turned and walked away without another word.

As Archie and his uncle boarded the steamship, Archie fumbled with the gift. A pair of tightly tied drawstrings held the pouch together.

Archie undid the strings and upended the pouch. A nugget of gold wrapped in a slip of paper tumbled out into his waiting palm. Not just any nugget of gold either. It was the one Archie had found the day before. He could even see the *V* Val had carved into it.

The slip of paper contained a note scribbled in ink. It read: *Hope you find your way home safe, new kid.*

Archie smiled and held the nugget tight. He knew just what Val meant. He couldn't wait to pick out a new fiddle when they arrived back in Seattle.

The steamship pulled away from the harbor. Archie stood at the boat's rail, his eyes on Dawson City, until it was nothing more than a speck.

One adventure complete. A new one just beyond the horizon.

THE HISTORY BEHIND THE KLONDIKE GOLD RUSH

The Klondike (or Yukon) Gold Rush began when George Washington Carmack and his Taglish Indian companions discovered gold in the Canadian Yukon Territory on August 16, 1896. The find occurred on Rabbit Creek (later renamed Bonanza Creek), a tributary of the Klondike River. When news returned to the United States of the gold strike, many eager men and women headed north to try their hand at gaining fortune. They became known as the "stampeders."

Reaching the Yukon was dangerous. Canadian authorities required each person to take with them one year's worth of mining equipment and supplies, such as boots and outerwear, medicine and first-aid items, soap, and nearly one thousand pounds of food. The journey required stampeders to travel along one of two trails: the White Pass Trail from Skagway, Alaska, or the Chilkoot Trail from Dyea, Alaska. Many did not survive this portion of the trip, either turning back or losing their lives to events such as avalanches. Upon reaching the end of the trails at Lake Bennett, any would-be prospector needed to build his or her own boat and take it five hundred miles down the treacherous Yukon River to a town called Dawson City.

In 1896, when gold was first discovered, Dawson City was a small town of five hundred. But by 1898 it had expanded to house nearly thirty thousand people. Miners who arrived in the winter had to wait for the ground to thaw to begin mining. This meant the town saw huge growth, with the opening of saloons, supply stores, banks, and restaurants. Many stampeders who found gold in the region spent it in Dawson City.

The discovery of gold in the Yukon made a few lucky miners rich. Many, however, left there empty-handed. In 1898, construction began on the White Pass & Yukon Railroad, a steam engine that offered travelers an alternative to the harsh, difficult Chilkoot and White Trail Passes. But it didn't open until after the Klondike Gold Rush had reached its peak.

In the summer of 1899, gold was discovered around Nome, Alaska. Many disappointed prospectors left the Klondike, hoping their luck would change in a new location. This was the end of the Klondike gold rush. While mining activity during the rush lasted until 1903, the Klondike continues to be occasionally mined for more gold. All in all, it is estimated that fourteen million ounces of gold has been taken from the area.

GLOSSARY

avalanche (A-vuh-lanch)—a large mass of snow and ice that has become detached from a mountain slope and is suddenly sliding or falling downward

canteen (kan-TEEN)—a small container used for carrying water or other liquids

kerosene (KER-uh-seen)—a thin liquid fuel; kerosene is usually made from petroleum, but can also be made from coal, oil, or tar

mercantile (MUR-ken-teel)—a store, typically in a small town, selling a wide variety of goods

outcropping (OUT-krop-ing)—a section of rock above the soil that extends outward

parcel (PAR-sell)—a piece of land that is part of a larger piece

pitch (PICH)—thick, sticky tar used for patching holes in a ship's hull

prospector (PRAH-spekt-ore)—a person who searches for precious minerals and metals

provisions (proh-VI-shuns)—a supply of food or goods

riffles (RIF-uhls)—the lining of bars on the bed of a sluice, set up to catch minerals like gold

sabotage (SA-buh-tahj)—damage done to property in secret in order to stop some activity

SOURDOUGH RECIPE

A prospector who survived the harsh Yukon winter was commonly nicknamed a "sourdough." Prospectors lived on little food, including sourdough bread and pancakes. The tradition of making sourdough continues in the Yukon Territory to this day.

Ingredients for Pancakes

- 2 cups all-purpose flour
- 4 tsp. baking powder
- 1 tsp. baking soda
- 2 tbsp. granulated sugar
- 1 tsp. salt
- 1½ cups milk
- 1 egg (beaten)
- 2 tbsp. vegetable oil

To begin, make a sourdough starter.

In a nonmetal bowl, combine:

- 2 cups warm water heated to 95–100 degrees Fahrenheit (ask an adult to help)

- 1 package active dry yeast

- 2 cups all-purpose flour

- Loosely cover the bowl and let sit for 48 hours, stirring 2 to 3 times a day with a wooden spoon.

Directions

1. Whisk together flour, baking powder, baking soda, sugar, and salt.

2. To the dry mixture, add sourdough starter, milk, egg, and oils. Mix well.

3. Spray griddle with cooking spray. Heat to 300–350 degrees Fahrenheit.

4. Pour ¼ cup batter on the hot griddle. Cook until the pancake bubbles, then flip.

5. Cook for an additional minute, or until pancake is cooked through.

Serve with butter and syrup. Makes 10 servings.

Recipe courtesy of *Tastes of Lizzy T.*

ABOUT THE AUTHOR

Brandon Terrell is the author of numerous books and graphic novels, ranging from sports stories to spooky tales to mind-boggling mysteries. His work includes titles in the Jake Maddox chapter book and graphic novel series, several terrifying Spine Shivers and Michael Dahl Presents: Phobia tales, and the Snoops Inc. mystery series. When not hunched over his laptop writing, Brandon enjoys watching movies and TV, reading, watching baseball, cooking, and spending time with his wife and two children in Minnesota.

ABOUT THE ILLUSTRATOR

Eva Morales is a professional Spanish 2D artist and illustrator living near the Mediterranean Sea. She has worked in children's publishing, TV, film production, and advertising for about fourteen years. Now she works as a full-time freelance illustrator, using a combination of digital and traditional techniques. Eva loves to walk on the beach and read books in her spare time.